D1644991

Siar

Don Quixote

Adapted by
Mary Sebag Montefiore

Illustrated by Andy Catling

Reading consultant: Alison Kelly
Roehampton University

Contents

Chapter 1

Books are bad for you

Alonso Quixada had gone crazy – and quite suddenly. The priest and the barber, who were sitting with him in his library, sorrowfully shook their heads.

"Too much reading!" declared the priest.

"The wrong sort of books," added the barber. "Adventure stories indeed! And not just ordinary ones, but tales of witches, battles, haunted castles..."

Quixada's eyes shone like candles. "Haunted castles. *Yes!*"

"The trouble is you believe it all," said the priest. "You're really too old for stuff like that."

"And you have your housekeeper and your niece to look after you," the barber went on. "Why can't you be normal and contented like other people?"

"What a stupid question," Quixada thought, his face growing long with disgust. "It's not even worth an answer." He shoved them out of his library, sank into a chair and opened another book.

Knock, knock.

"What NOW?" he exclaimed irritably.

In marched his niece and housekeeper.
The housekeeper flicked her duster over
the bookshelves, sending spiders up in the
air and dust down her throat. "This room's
unhealthy," she choked. "Atishoo!"

"If only..." thought Quixada longingly,
completely ignoring them, "if only I, too,
could live like the brave knights of old.'

His niece dumped a tray on a table beside him. "Such nonsense! Here's your coffee. Drink it while it's hot."

"I'll do it!" cried Quixada, kicking the coffee away. "I will! I'll be famous... immortal! Watch me right the world's wrongs, kill dragons and rescue damsels in distress."

"Don't be silly," said his niece. "Spain doesn't have dragons... and here in La Mancha there are no damsels in distress."

"Oh yes there are!" Quixada roared, and he tore up to the attic.

An ancient iron suit lay on the floor. He scraped off the rust, cranked himself into it, waved a cracked shield and a dented lance, and jammed on the helmet.

"It's broken!" he mourned, but he was upset for only a moment. Resourcefully, he found some cardboard and made a visor, tied together with green ribbons. Then he rushed out to his decrepit old horse.

"You," he exclaimed, "my noble steed, shall be re-named Rocinante. But hang on! I need a grand name too. I'll call myself Don Quixote de la Mancha. Now, what else do I need for my adventure? A knight with no lady-love is like a tree without leaves. Hmm..."

And then he remembered a pretty peasant girl in the village to whom he'd never spoken, called Aldonza. "I will dedicate myself to her," he decided. "And she shall be named Dulcinea del Toboso."

Rattling like a shelf of crooked saucepans, he mounted Rocinante and trotted away. "O Dulcinea, my Princess, remember me!" he murmured, as if he'd really been in love.

He rode until nightfall when, exhausted and starving, a terrible thought made him pull up his reins. Rocinante juddered to a halt. "I haven't been knighted yet! Someone must do it – and quickly!"

Chapter 2

A hard day for a knight

Don Quixote had reached a dirty wayside inn where dung-spattered straw blew around the yard, making it stink. From the fields, a swineherd sounded his horn to gather his pigs.

"This," Don Quixote told himself, "is a great castle with a moat and towers. Hark! A magnificent trumpet blast is announcing my arrival. Sir," he asked the innkeeper, "are you governor of this noble castle?"

"He's crazy," thought the innkeeper. "And he's a strange man, with his odd, long face. But I'd better not upset him... Er, the governor?" he said. "Yes I am."

"Then take my horse to your stable, and let me rest here tonight after something to eat. But first, get me out of my suit."

The innkeeper unstrapped the buckles and dropped the suit by a water trough, but he couldn't undo the cardboard visor without untying the ribbons.

"Don't touch my helmet!" ordered Don Quixote, afraid it would all fall apart.

"That makes things difficult..." hesitated the innkeeper. "If you want to eat, you'll have to hold the visor open so I can drop food in your mouth. And I'll have to pour in your drink."

As Don Quixote munched his supper in this unusual manner, a muleteer led his mule to the water trough, tripped over Quixote's shield, and hurled it aside.

"Help me, sweet Dulcinea, in this first moment of peril!" whispered Don Quixote. Jumping up, he clonked the muleteer on the head. "You dare to lay one finger on my shield!" he shouted. "You'll pay for it with your life!"

The man fell down, stunned. A second man rushed to help, but Don Quixote hit him too. With two bodies lying senseless in the yard, all the people staying in the inn raced outside and began throwing stones at Don Quixote.

"Vile cowards!" yelled Don Quixote. "Base-born rabble. Come nearer, I'll stand up to you. You'll pay for your insolence."

He sounded so fierce that they stopped. The wounded men were taken away, leaving Don Quixote bruised but triumphant. "Now I have proved my bravery, will you perform the deed of knighthood?" Don Quixote asked the astonished innkeeper.

"I'd better get on with it before there are any more calamities," he thought and, taking Don Quixote's sword, he touched each shoulder, proclaiming: "I name you Knight of the Long Face. May God make you a fortunate knight and give you luck in your battles."

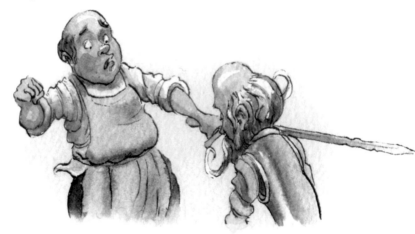

Eager to see the back of him, he added, "I'm not going to charge you for supper, so you can leave first thing in the morning."

"Charge me?" exclaimed Don Quixote. "Money isn't mentioned in any of the adventure books I've read."

"Ah," said the innkeeper, trying hard to avoid another outburst. "Most knights have squires who keep supplies in their saddlebags – money, clean shirts, ointment to cure wounds and so on."

Don Quixote rubbed himself where the stones had hurt him. "What a good idea."

As he jogged away on Rocinante's scrawny back, his brain sizzled with decision. "Now I'm the Knight of the Long Face, I must get myself a squire."

Chapter 3

Treacherous windmills

"Don't go away again," begged his niece when he got home. "You're ill! Believing you're a knight – it's ridiculous!"

"Let me get back to my books," urged Don Quixote. "*They're* not ridiculous."

But it was too late. While he'd been away, his housekeeper had made a huge bonfire and burned them all. The priest and the barber had walled up the library door, so he couldn't even find his empty shelves. Furiously, he felt over the place where the door used to be. At last, worn out with raving, he went to bed.

18

The following morning, he crept out secretly to sell some land to pay for his next adventure. On the way back, he met Sancho Panza, a farmer who lived nearby.

"You can't miss the opportunity of being my squire," said Don Quixote in his most persuasive voice. "Just think what glittering prizes you might win with me: money, treasure, land... If I conquer an island, which could easily happen, I'll make you governor."

"Oh," gulped Sancho Panza. He grinned.

"We'll set off this very night!" decided Don Quixote. "Don't forget saddle bags and don't tell a soul."

That evening, Sancho Panza, with the bags and a leather bottle strapped to his donkey, rode proudly next to Don Quixote. Crossing a huge plain, they espied thirty or forty windmills in the distance.

"Look!" shouted Don Quixote. "Over there – thirty or more terrible giants whom I will fight and kill."

"Giants? Where?" asked Sancho Panza.

"Over there," pointed Don Quixote, "with the long arms. These giants have arms almost six miles long."

"Those aren't giants," Sancho retorted. "They're windmills. What you think are

arms are in fact their sails. When the wind turns them, they turn millstones."

"You don't know anything about adventures," replied Don Quixote. "They're giants, and if you're frightened, you can hide and say your prayers while I fight them." He sank his spurs into Rocinante and charged them at top speed, calling as he galloped,

"Help me, sweet Dulcinea..."

"Flee not, you evil creatures," he cried. "Only one brave knight attacks you!"

A gust of wind arose and the sails began to move. Don Quixote shrieked, "But you have more arms than any giant should have, and I will make you pay for that."

He thrust his lance into a sail, but the wind turned the sail so fast, it smashed the lance to smithereens, dragging the horse and his rider with it. Don Quixote went rolling over the plain with yelps of pain.

Sancho Panza prodded his donkey and rushed to help. "Didn't I tell you to be careful? Didn't I say they were windmills?"

"You don't understand," Don Quixote replied, struggling back onto his horse. "An evil enchanter has just turned all these giants into windmills to deprive me of my glorious victory."

"And now you're riding all lopsided," Sancho observed.

"I know." Don Quixote, wincing, tried to sit straighter. "But do I moan? Never! Knights aren't allowed to grumble, no matter how severe their wounds."

"I'm glad I'm only a squire, not a knight," said Sancho, swigging a drink from his leather bottle. "I'm going to moan like anything if I get hurt."

Don Quixote wasn't listening. He tore off a dead branch from an oak tree. "This will be my new lance," he cried, fixing on the iron head from the broken one. "We'll spend the night under these trees and see what happens tomorrow."

Chapter 4

Deceitful sheep

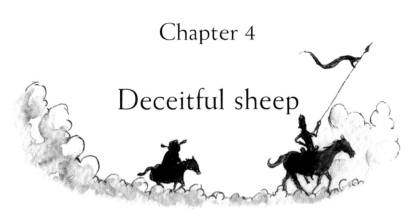

In the morning, after breakfast, Don Quixote noticed a huge, dense cloud of dust approaching them along the road. He almost purred with delight. "See that, Sancho? My great deeds today will be written in the book of fame for future generations to admire. That dust is coming from a vast army of countless different nations marching towards us."

"In that case there must be two armies," said Sancho. "Because opposite it, back there behind us, is another dust cloud, just like it."

Turning around, Don Quixote saw that Sancho was right. "These two armies," he proclaimed, "will clash in the middle of this vast plain. The army in front is led by the great Emperor Alifanfarón; the army coming up behind belongs to his enemy, Pentapolin, King of the Garamentes."

"Why do these two lords hate each other so much?" asked Sancho.

"Because..." replied Don Quixote, thinking rapidly. He could picture the scenario so clearly, he was convinced it was real. "This Alifanfarón loves King Pentapolin's daughter, and the King won't let them marry because Alifanfarón is a pagan, and Pentapolin's a Christian."

As the dust clouds loomed ever larger, Don Quixote, more excited by the minute, even began naming the knights in each army, pointing out their flags. "Listen, Sancho. Can't you hear the horses, the bugles, the beating of the drums?"

"All I hear," said Sancho, "is lots of
sheep bleating." He was right. Two flocks
of sheep were coming closer, flanked
by shepherds.

"You're too scared to see properly,"
scoffed Don Quixote. "Stand aside while
I support one of these armies."

He whipped up old Rocinante into a
gallop, waved his lance and sped across
the plain like a thunderbolt.

"Come back!" yelled Sancho. "I swear by my sword it's sheep you're charging."

"Follow me, knights of the Emperor!" cried Don Quixote, ignoring Sancho as he galloped straight into the army of sheep, spearing them with fury. "I am the Knight of the Long Face."

"Stop!" shrieked the shepherds. When they found Don Quixote was unstoppable, they drew out their slings and pelted him with stones until he fell down, squealing with agony. Quickly, they rounded up their flocks and raced away.

"Are you badly wounded?" panted Sancho, running as fast as he could to where Don Quixote lay.

"I think they've knocked all my teeth out." Don Quixote staggered stiffly to his feet. "But knights never complain. I'd rather lose teeth than my sword arm."

"Didn't I tell you they were sheep?"

"It just shows," replied Don Quixote, "my old enemy, the enchanter, is up to his tricks again. Envious of the glory that was just a breath away from being mine, he turned the armies into a flock of sheep. I was on the knife-edge of victory. Never mind, Sancho. Another adventure awaits us on another day."

Chapter 5

The sour fruit of freedom

The very next day, as Don Quixote and Sancho Panza trotted down the road, they passed twelve men walking in a line, strung by the neck like beads on a great iron chain, with shackles on their hands. Accompanying them were two men on horseback and another two on foot.

"Look – a chain gang of prisoners on their forced march to the sea. They're off to be galley slaves, roped to the oars to row the King's ships," remarked Sancho.

"WHAT?" thundered Don Quixote. "You mean they're being forced, against their will, to march to slavery? How can the King allow it?"

"It's not like that," Sancho tried to explain. "They're criminals. They've done very bad things. This is their punishment."

"Whatever the rights and wrongs, this is a situation that calls for ME. The relief of the wretched. The redressing of outrage."

"Leave them alone," advised Sancho.

"I'll have a word with them first," said Quixote. "What did you do?" he asked one of the chained-up men.

"I was a horse thief," replied the prisoner.

"And you?" he turned to another.

"I stole some wine."

"What about you?" he asked a third.

"Be quick," snarled a guard, threatening the prisoner with his stick. "This one's a dangerous villain who's committed more terrible crimes than the rest of this gang."

"You weren't given that stick to ill-treat us," this prisoner retorted boldly. "My name is Pasamonte. I've been in worse places than this and escaped... I'm no coward. Let's just get on with what must be done and make no fuss about it."

"I've heard enough!" shouted Don Quixote, moved by these brave words. "Guards, these poor men haven't done any harm to you. Let them go."

The guards split their sides laughing. "This man's a lunatic," they cackled. "Come on. Joke over."

"It's not a joke," cried Don Quixote, hitting one of the guards. Taken by surprise, the guard fell to the ground.

"Stop!" screamed the remaining guards, surrounding Don Quixote menacingly.

Sancho drew his sword. Though he was frightened, he slashed away so fiercely that the guards fled, terrified for their lives.

Quickly the prisoners seized their opportunity and smashed the chain that imprisoned them.

"I've given you and your friends freedom, Pasamonte," Don Quixote exulted. "In return, do one thing for me. Go at once to my Lady, Dulcinea del Toboso, and tell her every detail of this adventure, so she knows how valiant I've been."

"Don't be so daft," Pasamonte replied. "Of course I won't. I'm not hanging around for you or the Holy Brotherhood."

"The Holy Who?" asked Sancho.

"The police, you ignorant oaf. They'll be looking for us now and they're vicious. I'd better disguise myself... I know: I'll steal your clothes!"

Pasamonte snatched the coat Don Quixote had on, stripped off Sancho's hat and stockings and cleared off as fast as he could. The other prisoners had already disappeared.

"Ungrateful wretches!" yelled Don Quixote, shaking his fist to the empty air.

"Oh dear," shivered Sancho, his bare knees knocking together. "That horrible Holy Brotherhood will be after us too, for setting them free. We'd better go."

Don Quixote swung himself onto Rocinante's back. "How could they treat us so badly, when we did so much for them?" he asked, bewildered.

For once Sancho had no answer.

Chapter 6

Mad with passion

Don Quixote and Sancho forged their way through forest ravines up to the lonely mountains to hide from the police.

"At least those rapscallion prisoners didn't pinch our saddle bags with all our food," said Sancho, peering inside them. "Salami and wine. Yum. Let's sit down and have lunch." Then he added, quaking, "I hope the bears don't get us."

"This is the perfect place for an adventure, Greedy-guts, not a picnic," said Don Quixote. "All my books feature knights wandering in wild mountains."

Daydreaming happily, Don Quixote noticed a bag disintegrating under a pile of leaves. "Quick, Sancho!" he called. "What's this?"

"Ooh!" squealed Sancho, ripping the rotten leather open. "Four fine shirts. Lots of gold coins. And a dirty old notebook. Someone's written a silly poem. Listen." He read aloud:

> *Where gods are cruel and love is blind*
> *Misery has pierced my mind...*
> *Let me die, for I am sure*
> *Without Lucinda, there's no cure.*

"Aha," said Don Quixote. "It's obvious what this is all about. A knight has been rejected by his love and has come here to die in his loneliness. I have to admit, though, knights are more noted for their bravery than the elegance of their verse. Why don't you take the money, Sancho, and keep it for yourself? I don't want it."

"At last! An adventure that pays cash!" exclaimed Sancho, stuffing the coins into his own saddle bags. "Hey, what's over there?" He pointed in the distance where a wild man, half naked, with a thick beard and a pony tail, leaped over rocks.

"Our poet, I expect," Don Quixote said. "Let's follow him."

"N-No," murmured Sancho, "because then I might have to give this lovely money back."

"Well, yes," Don Quixote replied. "Or you'll be guilty of stealing."

"But he looks crazy," Sancho moaned. "I don't suppose he wants it."

"You should ask him. Do your duty, and hold your head up high."

They soon caught up with the wild man who greeted them politely, and then cried, "If you people have anything to eat, for God's sake, let me have it."

"Poor, ravenous Ragged Knight," Don Quixote whispered. "Sir, my whole desire is to help you," he said courteously. "All that is mine, consider yours. Eat your fill and tell me, who are you and what brought you here to this wilderness?"

After eating, the Ragged Knight stretched himself out on the grass. "This is my story. Don't interrupt, please. I'd like to get it over quickly since to dwell on my misfortunes is to add to them."

"I promise," said Don Quixote, sitting beside him. "And so does Sancho."

"I am Cardenio, a nobleman from Andalusia. I have loved Lucinda from childhood, and she loved me. I asked, and was granted, her father's permission to marry her. Then I received a letter from Duke Ricardo, the most powerful noble in Spain, demanding my services as companion to his son, Fernando.

I left my home and Lucinda to earn gold for her. Fernando and I became friends. He is young, handsome, fun. I told him about Lucinda, her beauty, wit and intelligence and he..."

Cardenio broke down, weeping, before forcing himself to continue. "He betrayed our friendship. He sought out Lucinda and, as his family is richer and grander than mine, he easily persuaded her father that he, not I, should be her husband."

"Shocking!" exclaimed Don Quixote.

"He married her. He stole her from me, though he was already engaged to be married to Dorotea." With these words, Cardenio drummed his feet and waved his arms in circles. "Agh!" he screamed and flattened Don Quixote with his fists.

"Uh-oh, he's going crazy. Better get out of here," Sancho advised, jumping on his donkey. Don Quixote staggered into his stirrups, and they rode away.

Cardenio, howling with misery, ran off and disappeared between the shadowy mountain peaks.

"It makes you think, Sancho," Don Quixote said. "Fernando's treachery... I don't want anyone stealing my Lady Dulcinea from me. Pen and paper, please."

Sancho got them out of his saddle bag and watched as Don Quixote scribbled:

Noble Lady,
Sweetest Dulcinea del Toboso
If your beautiful self scorns me, my life is not worth living. Say you will be mine, or I will end it – to satisfy your cruelty and my desire.
Your Own,
Knight of the Long Face

"A very good letter," said Sancho, buckling up his saddle bag and smacking it with satisfaction, stuffed as it was with the Ragged Knight's coins.

Sancho had no intention of finding Dulcinea. Instead he planned to ride straight to the nearest inn and order a large hot dinner. He was tired of snacking on cold food. "What will you eat while I'm gone?" he asked Don Quixote, feeling a twinge of guilt.

"Fruit from the trees," Quixote replied. "I will be half-naked and miserable, like Cardenio. I've learned a lot about knightly conduct from him. Take Rocinante. Tie your donkey to his harness; you'll get there faster."

So saying, Don Quixote ripped his shirt in two and began to wander, carving poems onto the bark of trees.

HE SOUGHT ADVENTURES
AS HE PINED
FOR HIS QUEEN,
WHOSE EYES ARE BLIND.

Chapter 7

Costumes and confusion

When Sancho reached an inn, he was surprised to see the priest and the barber from his own village.

"Where's Don Quixote?" they demanded. "You've got his horse."

Sancho explained the terrible effect of Cardenio's story on Don Quixote. "Here's his letter to Dulcinea." He searched in the saddle bags and turned his pockets inside out. "Oh no! I've lost it."

"She hasn't a clue who he is anyway,"
said the priest, "so that doesn't matter.
What does matter is getting him home."

"How...?" mused the barber.

"Suppose..." said the priest thoughtfully,
"I dress up as a girl and pretend to be a
damsel in distress. You," he pointed to the
barber, "pretend to be my squire. You must
ask Quixote to save me from a wicked
knight, by taking me to a secret destination,
without asking questions. Then we can
whisk him back home."

"Brilliant!" said the barber.

The innkeeper's wife lent them a dress,
and the barber created a beard from a cow's
tail. The priest looked as pretty as a picture.

"Oh dear," he said, gazing in the glass. "I look unsuitable for a man in my profession. Let's swap."

The barber agreed. Now he looked as pretty as a picture, and the priest wore the cow's tail beard.

Sancho guided them towards the spot where he'd left Don Quixote. They stopped by a river, stumbling over Cardenio, who was amazed that the priest and barber knew his story from Sancho.

"Listen... can you hear singing?" asked the priest.

A young boy in farmer's clothes was paddling in the river shallows, singing a sad song in a sweet voice.

"Look at his hands!" whispered the barber.

"I see what you mean," the priest replied softly. "Small and white as alabaster. That's a girl in disguise."

"Almost as lovely as Lucinda," blurted Cardenio as the boy displayed a face of extraordinary beauty.

"My Lady... for surely you are a lady, do you need help?" offered the priest.

The beauty instantly burst into tears. "No one can help me. I am Dorotea, from Andalusia. I was going to be married, but Fernando, my beloved, jilted me for a girl from a noble family, unlike poor me."

"Fernando!" Cardenio gulped.

"I raced to make him marry me. I love him still. But I was too late. I discovered that his bride, Lucinda, had fainted during the wedding, while taking her vows. Just before she fell unconscious, she declared she loved Cardenio. She only agreed to wed Fernando because her parents had forced her and she swore to kill herself with a dagger.

The priest dissolved the marriage and Fernando rode off in a rage. Cardenio had already disappeared. I ran away, too miserable to start a new life, and wandered into these mountains."

"I am Cardenio," that man declared. "I won't rest until I see you married to Fernando, while I..." He flung his arms up to the sky with joy. "I will marry my lovely Lucinda. My madness is cured."

"Excellent," said the priest. "Now we must look after Don Quixote."

"The famous, crazy knight?" Dorotea was so happy, knowing she would be reunited with Fernando, that she wanted to make all the world happy too. Hearing Don Quixote's predicament, she turned to the barber. "Lend me your pretty dress. I have an idea..."

Chapter 8

Demons in the ox cart

Don Quixote sat under a tree, half-naked, his clothes dangling from a branch above.

Dorotea threw herself at his feet. "Are you the Knight of the Long Face?" she asked. "I am Princess Mircomicona. A giant has stolen my land and threatens to eat my father. Can you help me?"

"A beautiful damsel in distress?" responded Quixote warmly. "I'll do everything I can for you."

"Will you promise not to get involved in any other adventure until you've sorted mine out?" pleaded Dorotea.

"I swear," answered Don Quixote. "Sancho, help me with my suit."

Hidden behind another tree, the barber laughed so much that his beard fell off. Quickly he stuck it back. Cardenio was disguised in the priest's hooded cloak, while the priest – strutting uncloaked in his doublet and hose – was unrecognizable. They followed Don Quixote, Sancho and Dorotea across the plain to the inn.

"Don't get upset with the man in the suit," the priest told the innkeeper. "'He's crazy but harmless."

"I heard the Holy Brotherhood want him."

"Please don't tell them," begged the priest. "We're taking him home."

"He can sleep in the barn loft where I keep my wine. Out of harm's way," the innkeeper replied kindly.

At midnight Sancho screamed, waking the entire inn. "Come quickly! My master's fighting... There's blood everywhere..."

"EVIL CREATURE!" Don Quixote yelled, brandishing his sword.

"He's slashed my wineskins," roared the innkeeper in fury, looking at the floor awash with a lake of red bubbles. "My best vintage, ruined!"

"I've killed Princess Mircomicona's giant," Don Quixote triumphed. "It was a fierce battle, and I won."

"You've wounded wineskins," scolded the innkeeper. "As you'll realize when you get my bill."

"This room is too sodden with blood to sleep in," yawned Don Quixote wearily. "I'll go downstairs."

In the hall two ghostly figures with white faces and dark cloaks seized him, dragged him to the courtyard, and threw him in a wooden cage which they hoisted onto an ox cart. Sancho found himself tossed beside his master. There they sat, bruised and dazed, clutching the bars of their prison.

"Knight of the Long Face," chorused scary voices. "An enchanter sends you and your squire into the unknown. He asks you to promise to go on no more adventures for a year. Do you swear?"

"Y...Yes," quavered Don Quixote.

"Then we'll leave you."

"I never read of transport like this in my books," Don Quixote complained to Sancho. "Knights are usually whisked off on magic carpets. But I'll do as that enchanter says."

The demons grinned. "It's worked," they chortled, jiggling the ox cart reins. The priest and the barber took off their cloaks and scrubbed the paste from their faces. They were taking Don Quixote home to La Mancha.

Chapter 9

Farewell good knight

Don Quixote woke up to find himself back in his own bed.

His niece and housekeeper, overcome with relief, constantly brought him tempting trays of food and drink.

"Thank goodness you're safe. We've been so worried," they chorused.

Don Quixote felt curiously weak, now that he was not expending all his energy on adventures. He stayed in bed, remembering how he had wandered in search of danger with Rocinante and Sancho Panza.

Sancho came to visit him. "Someone's written a book about you," he announced. "Look... You're famous, just as you wanted."

"Let me see," Don Quixote flicked the pages. It was a big book, with illustrations of the knight on Rocinante, dwarfing Sancho and his donkey, tilting at windmills, charging over the wide Spanish plains.

"I'm not sure about it," Sancho said. "It makes you out to be a figure of fun. It's easy to ridicule, harder to be fair, especially when the truth is not obvious. The Don Quixote I know is brave, wise and kind – righter of wrongs, a protector... This Don Quixote, the one in print, is a mockery."

"I don't feel very well," yawned Don Quixote, sinking back into his pillow. Just before he fell asleep he muttered, "I'd like to see a doctor, a lawyer and the priest. I think I'm going to die."

"He's suffering from melancholy," said the doctor, when he came. He felt Don Quixote's pulse. It was very low.

His friends gathered around. "We must help him," they insisted.

But there was nothing they could do. Don Quixote was fast asleep, and they feared he would never wake up.

At last he did.

"I must make my will," he announced with a smidgen of his old energy. "I am no longer Don Quixote de la Mancha, but rather Alonso Quixada. I was mad; now I am sane. So near death, I will not joke about names or noble deeds."

Sancho was unashamedly in floods of tears. "Get up... Let's go on adventures again and have fun. Don't die of grief – it isn't worth it. A disappointed knight today is a conqueror tomorrow."

Don Quixote hardly listened. "I leave you a sum of money, Sancho, so that you can lead a good and useful life. My house-keeper shall likewise have money... and to my niece, I leave all my household goods, with the proviso that if she marries a man who has a library of adventure books, she forfeits all that is mine."

With these words, Don Quixote closed his eyes and breathed his last.

That was the end of the Knight of the Long Face. His friends had an epitaph carved on his tombstone.

Don Quixote

He never cared what
people thought –
A clown to pompous eyes.
He lived his life a gallant fool
And finally died wise.

Miguel de Cervantes Saavedra
1547-1616

Miguel de Cervantes Saavedra had a life as full of adventure as his hero: he was a soldier and wounded in battle; he was kidnapped by pirates and spent five years as a slave.

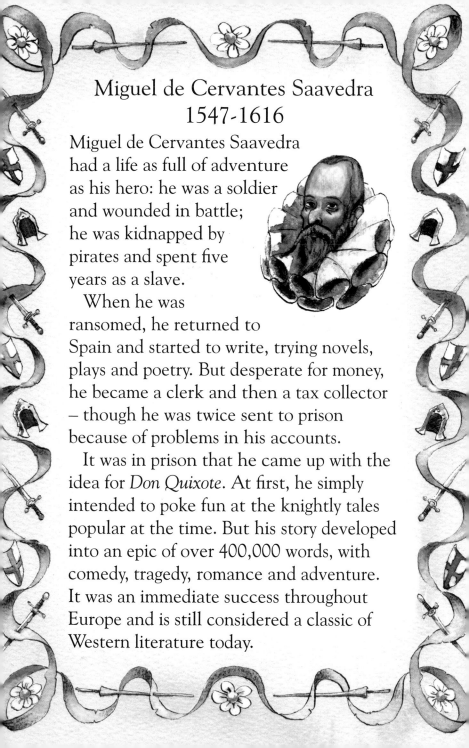

When he was ransomed, he returned to Spain and started to write, trying novels, plays and poetry. But desperate for money, he became a clerk and then a tax collector – though he was twice sent to prison because of problems in his accounts.

It was in prison that he came up with the idea for *Don Quixote*. At first, he simply intended to poke fun at the knightly tales popular at the time. But his story developed into an epic of over 400,000 words, with comedy, tragedy, romance and adventure. It was an immediate success throughout Europe and is still considered a classic of Western literature today.

Designed by Michelle Lawrence
Digital manipulation: Nick Wakeford
Series designer: Russell Punter
Series editor: Lesley Sims

First published in 2010 by Usborne Publishing Ltd.,
Usborne House, 83-85 Saffron Hill, London
EC1N 8RT, England.
www.usborne.com

UE. First published in America in 2010.